REMARKABLE CHILDREN

MARY ANNING

THE FOSSIL HUNTER

A Picture-Book Biography

*The information for the Remarkable Children Series was
gathered from old letters, journals, and other historical documents.*

For My Wife, Judy Fradin, With Love.
D.F.

To my favorite fossil-hunter, my dear wife Carol
T.N.

Text copyright ©1998 by Dennis Fradin
Illustrations copyright © 1998 by Tom Newsom
Photo credits: Photo Research by Susan Van Etten; p. 32, all, ©The Natural History
Museum, London, England; back cover, ©The Natural History Museum, London, England.

Published by Silver Press
A Division of Simon & Schuster
299 Jefferson Road, Parsippany, NJ 07054

Designed by Brooks Design

Printed in the United States of America

ISBN 0-382-39486-0 (LSB) 10 9 8 7 6 5 4 3 2 1
ISBN 0-382-39487-9 (pbk) 10 9 8 7 6 5 4 3 2 1

Library of Congress Cataloging-in-Publication Data
Fradin, Dennis B.
Mary Anning, fossil hunter/by Dennis Fradin: illustrated by Tom Newsom.
p. cm. — (Remarkable children series: #3)
Summary: A biography of the young English girl who made a major fossil discovery at
age eleven and grew up to be one of the world's foremost fossil hunters.
1. Anning, Mary, 1799-1847—Juvenile literature. 2. Paleontologists—England—Biography—
Juvenile literature. (1. Anning, Mary, 1799-1847. 2. Paleontologists. 3. Women—Biography)
I. Newsom, Tom, ill. II. Title. III. Series.
QE707.A56F73 1997
96-17834 560'.9—dc20 CIP AC

REMARKABLE CHILDREN

MARY ANNING

THE FOSSIL HUNTER

The true story of an English girl who made a major fossil discovery at the age of 11 and grew up to be one of the world's foremost fossil hunters.

BY DENNIS FRADIN • ILLUSTRATED BY TOM NEWSOM

Silver Press
Parsippany, New Jersey

Mary Anning was born on May 21, 1799, in Lyme Regis, a seaside town in southern England. She grew up to be a famous collector of fossils, which are remains of ancient plants and animals, but she almost didn't get to grow up at all. Just after Mary's first birthday, a friend took her to see a horseback riding show in a farm pasture. A rainstorm ended the show and scattered the crowd. "It thundered and lightninged to such a degree," a witness reported, "as not remembered by the oldest person in the town."

While most of the crowd hid in some storage sheds, the woman holding Mary joined a few other people beneath a large elm tree. She couldn't have picked a more dangerous spot. Suddenly, a lightning bolt hit the tree, killing two teenage girls and the Annings' family friend. Mary was burned by the lightning and seemed to have stopped breathing. Only after she was carried home to her parents did she finally open her eyes. A family legend was begun that "Mary had been a dull child before, but after this accident she became lively and intelligent." Of course being hit by lightning can't really make a person smarter. However, similar storms

did help Mary make some great discoveries in the years to come.

Mary lived with her older brother Joseph and their parents on Bridge Street, only about 50 feet from the sea. Mr. Anning made cabinets and other furniture in his carpentry shop near the town jail. Although far from rich, the Annings managed to get by—until the night a flood wrecked their house.

Mr. Anning rebuilt the cottage. But the repairs were so costly that he needed to find a way to increase his income. In the early 1800's, people were becoming interested in fossils, which were known as "curiosities" at that time. On his days off, Mr. Anning began collecting fossils along the nearby sea cliffs and beaches. Each day at school, Mary looked forward to the weekend when she and Joseph joined their father on his fossil hunts. The day after a storm was Mary's favorite time to go, for the wind and water would rip away at the cliffs, sometimes exposing bones that had been buried for millions of years. Together, Mr. Anning and his children found fossil fish, as well as spiral-shaped shells of ancient sea creatures called ammonites.

Besides being rich in fossils, Lyme Regis was a popular vacation resort when Mary was a child. Each summer, visitors flocked there from London and other cities to enjoy the sea air and splash in the ocean. The tourists liked to buy unusual gifts to bring home. All year the Annings collected fossils, which Mary and Joseph sold from a table outside their father's carpentry shop in the summertime. Mary felt proud whenever someone bought a curiosity she had found, for the money meant a lot to her family.

In 1810, the Annings suffered a tragedy when Mary's father died of tuberculosis. On top of their grief, the three remaining members of the family faced another problem—they were suddenly poor. Eleven-year-old Mary had to quit school because her mother could no longer afford to send her. Fourteen-year-old Joseph found a job covering chairs, but his salary was so small that at times the Annings went hungry.

Mary continued to hunt for curiosities following her father's death. At first she did this just to recall the happy times when her father was alive. Then, one day at the beach, she found a beautiful ammonite. As Mary

was walking home, a woman stopped her to look at the 200-million-year-old fossil shell in her hand. "I will give you a half crown for it," said the lady. As Mary exchanged the shell for the coin, she knew she had found a way to help support her family.

She regularly went down to the ocean to search for curiosities after that. The girl climbing about the cliffs with her basket over her arm and her hammer in her hand became a familiar sight to the people of Lyme Regis. Mary sold her curiosities from a table outside her family's cottage. Small though it was at first, Mary's curiosity business helped buy food for the household.

Now and then on holidays, Joseph went down to the beach with his sister. He also collected fossils by himself on occasion. Within a few months of Mr. Anning's death, Joseph discovered a giant fossil skull. People who saw him carrying it through the streets thought it must have belonged to a prehistoric crocodile. Mary thought the same thing when her brother reached home with the huge skull.

Mary had Joseph take her to the spot where he had found the skull. The two of them chipped away at the

cliffside but found no trace of the rest of the skeleton. Over the next few weeks, Mary continued the search without success. If the creature's bones were there, they were too deep inside the cliff for her to dig out.

Then one night in early 1811, a storm battered Lyme Regis. Mary Anning may have been the only person in town who enjoyed it. Her excitement grew with every flash of lightning that lit the sky and each wave that crashed against the shore. Mary fell asleep hoping that the storm would accomplish what she hadn't been able to do with her shovel and hammer.

Early the next morning, Mary raced down to the beach. The moment she reached the spot, she saw it— a gigantic skeleton sticking out of the cliffside. Mary took her tools from the basket and began to loosen the dirt from the bones. But the skeleton was too big for the eleven-year-old girl to dig out by herself.

Mary ran back into town where she found a group of workmen willing to help. The men followed her to the cliff and were about to dig out the skeleton with their shovels when Mary had a better idea. So that the bones wouldn't be damaged, she told them to dig out

the entire block of rock containing the skeleton. When the men held up the rock, Mary saw that the skeleton was truly monstrous—about 20 feet in length.

The people of Lyme Regis then watched a strange procession pass through town. A young girl led it, followed by workmen carrying a huge skeleton in a slab of rock. Mary led the men to her house on Bridge Street and knocked on the door. We can imagine Mrs. Anning's surprise when she opened the door and saw a skeleton four times the length of her daughter.

The workmen could not squeeze the skeleton through the doorway, so Mary had them leave it on the street near her house. After paying the men, Mary fetched the skull that Joseph had found. It fit perfectly in the skeleton, like the final piece of a jigsaw puzzle.

Scientists throughout Europe soon learned that a fossil skeleton similar to that of a huge crocodile had been found in Lyme Regis, England. Some of them visited the Anning house to view the creature for themselves. They were amazed by the skeleton as well as by the fact that an eleven-year-old girl had discovered it with the help of her fourteen-year-old brother.

The scientists determined that the bones came from an animal far more unusual than a crocodile. Mary had found the first complete skeleton of a reptile resembling a huge fish that lived a hundred million years ago, during the age of the dinosaurs. At first, there was no scientific name for the creature, so people called it "Mary's Monster." Later it was named *Ichthyosaurus*, meaning "fish lizard."

Mary knew that she could not keep the skeleton in the street forever. But she didn't have to, for a rich man in Lyme Regis bought it from her for 23 pounds—quite a large sum in those days. The skeleton was later placed in the famous British Museum in London.

Many people expected Mary's interest in fossils to lessen with time but the opposite happened. When Mary was fourteen, a neighbor gave her a book about geology, which is the study of the earth's history. The book convinced her that she could collect fossils as a career. To geologists, fossils were not just curiosities, but clues that helped them learn about the animals and plants of long ago.

Mary Anning grew up to be one of the first people in the world to make a living collecting fossils. She continued to "fossilize," as she called fossil hunting, along the shore around Lyme Regis for the rest of her life. Much of that time, she was helped by an unusual assistant—one with four legs and a tail.

One day in about the year 1820, Mary was digging along the cliffs when a small black-and-white dog appeared at her side. When the dog followed her home that evening, Mary decided to keep him. She named him Tray, and he became so devoted to her that a portrait of Mary Anning drawn in her lifetime includes the little dog. Tray decided that his job was to protect Mary's fossils. Whenever she found a half-buried fossil bone, Tray sat on it and guarded it from people and seabirds until Mary was ready to dig it out.

Together, Mary and Tray found many ammonites and fish fossils. They also made several discoveries as remarkable as the *Ichthyosaurus* Mary had found at the age of eleven. In 1824, Mary Anning discovered the first almost-complete skeleton of a huge sea serpent that lived 200 million years ago. It was named

Plesiosaurus, meaning "lizard-like." Four years later, Mary uncovered the remains of a giant flying reptile that had soared through the skies 150 million years ago. Scientists called it a *Pterodactyl,* meaning "finger-winged." Her other major discoveries were a second *Ichthyosaurus* and a second *Plesiosaurus* skeleton.

Mary Anning earned enough money selling fossils to buy a large house on Broad Street for herself, Joseph, and their mother. Mary turned part of the house into a shop, where she sold her fossils. She placed an *Ichthyosaurus* skull and her most beautiful ammonite shells in her shop window to attract customers. On the inside, her shop had "hundreds of fossils piled about in the greatest disorder," according to dinosaur expert Dr. Gideon Mantell, one of the many geologists who bought fossils from her.

Few of the scientists she met impressed Mary Anning. For one thing, they used her fossils to win fame without giving her credit. "They suck my brains!" she complained to her friend Anna Maria Pinney. She told another friend, "I do so enjoy opposing the bigwigs!" meaning that she liked to argue about

geology with the scientists, many of whom expected to be treated like kings. Even real kings didn't impress Mary Anning. When the king of Saxony entered her shop, Mary let him know that *he* was fortunate to meet *her*. "I am well known throughout the whole of Europe!" she told him. Anna Maria Pinney wrote about Mary Anning in her journal: "She has the proudest and most unyielding spirit I have ever met with. She glories in being afraid of no one and in saying everything she pleases." Mrs. Anning coined a saying of her own to describe her daughter. "Mary is a history and a mystery," she would say, as the two of them worked in the fossil shop.

Mary Anning's favorite customers were the children of Lyme Regis. Joseph married in 1829 and, over the next few years, had five children. Mary Anning never married, yet she was often surrounded by children. Her shop became a meeting place for the town's young people. The children didn't have many pennies to spend, yet Mary spent countless hours showing them fossils and telling them about the days when *Pterodactyls* ruled the skies and dinosaurs walked

the earth. "The Fossil Woman," as the children called her, was also loved in Lyme Regis for her generosity. Anna Maria Pinney wrote in her journal that Mary often gave money to the needy and "attended the sick poor people of the town night and day."

Climbing about the beaches and cliffs was dangerous work. Several times while pursuing what she called her "passion for bones," Mary was nearly drowned by giant waves. Once when Anna Maria Pinney went fossil hunting with Mary, a huge wave suddenly rushed toward them. Anna Maria might have been swallowed up by the water if not for the bravery and strength of Mary Anning, who picked her up and carried her to safety. Landslides were another danger. Several times Mary and Tray were standing along a 100-foot-high cliff when a portion of it broke away and crashed into the sea below. The fossil hunter and her little black-and-white dog always managed to jump from the crumbling cliff to safety—until one day in 1833, when Tray was very old.

It happened while Mary and her dog were partway up a cliff. Suddenly Mary heard a loud noise. The next

second, a large chunk of the cliff came crashing down toward Mary and Tray. Mary leaped out of the way of the falling rocks, but Tray was killed. Mary deeply loved the dog who had been her constant companion during her fossil hunts for many years. In a letter, Mary wrote: "The death of my old faithful dog quite upset me. The cliff fell upon him and killed him in a moment before my eyes and close to my feet. It was but a moment between me and the same fate."

It was cancer that brought Mary Anning's life to an end in 1847 at the age of only forty-seven. Following her death, some scientists put up a plaque in her memory near the cliffs where she had hunted fossils for nearly all of her life. The plaque had important words on it about how Mary Anning had "furthered the science of geology." The children of Lyme Regis remembered Mary Anning by chanting a little rhyme about their friend "The Fossil Woman":

> Miss Anning, as a child, never passed
> A pin upon the ground;
> But picked it up, and so at last
> An *Ichthyosaurus* found.

REMINDERS OF MARY ANNING

Many fossils found by Mary Anning can be seen in the British Museum and in other museums around the world. Other reminders of Mary Anning include the flat spiral fossil shells called ammonites, which today are often used to make jewelry.

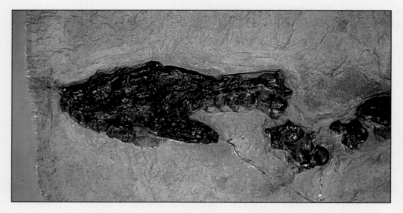

One of Mary Anning's greatest discoveries—the first jointed plesiosaur ever found.

Ammonites, flat spiral fossil shells, like the ones discovered by Mary Anning. Scientists use ammonites to tell how old a particular layer of rock is.

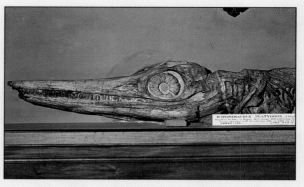

The skull of one of the ichthyosaurs collected by Mary Anning.